Our Snowman

OUR
SNOWMAN

o o o

M. B. Goffstein

Harper & Row, Publishers

New York

Our Snowman
Copyright © 1986 by M. B. Goffstein
Printed in U.S.A. All rights reserved.

Library of Congress Cataloging-in-Publication Data
Goffstein, M. B.
  Our snowman.

  "A Charlotte Zolotow book."
  Summary: The snowman two children build looks so
lonely when night comes that the little girl and her
father go out and make a snowman to keep him
company.
  [1. Snowman—Fiction]   I. Title.
PZ7.G55730u 1986   [E]   85-45836
ISBN 0-06-022152-6
ISBN 0-06-022153-4 (lib. bdg.)

Designed by Constance Fogler
1 2 3 4 5 6 7 8 9 10
First Edition

To my niece and nephew,
Sarah and Daniel Goffstein

After our first big blizzard
at the start of November,

we had below-zero weather,
and more snow fell every day.

Finally the sun came out.
The snow gleamed, heavy and sticky.

I zipped up my snowsuit in a hurry,
calling to my mother
to help get my little brother ready

to play out on our white lawn.

"The first thing we do," I told him, "is build a snowman."

I patted a snowball between my mittens,
and when I squatted down
and started rolling it to show him how,

we were both surprised
at the quick way it picked up
a thick covering of snow.

Year after year, these things work!

"The important thing," I told him,
"is to roll it in fresh places,
and not pick up mud or sticks."

He started rolling the bottom snowball,
while I went away to roll the middle—
and way away to roll the head.

We hoisted our snowman together,
and gave him a funny face.

Then my mother rapped on the window.
"Come in now," she called.

All during dinner I felt sad,
because our snowman stood alone
in the darkening night.

"We never should have made him,"
I said to my brother.

Then I couldn't eat dessert.

"You're going to have a hard life
if you cry over things like *that*,"
my mother warned me.

But suddenly my father and I
were dressing up warmly,

and my mother turned the porch light on.

My father rolled the bottom and the middle,

and I made the head.

I didn't dare tell *him*
not to pick up dirt or leaves,
so the snowman's wife got full of them,

but it looked like a pretty gown.

When we came inside again,
my brother was glad for me.

"Now they each have company," he said.